Tales for my dog

No, not – mostly – tales about dogs
Just stories about human beings
But any intelligent dog would understand
And in the end you will too...

David Heidenstam was born in Grimsby and grew up in Norfolk, England. Trained as a political scientist, he has worked as a labourer, security guard, park-keeper, editor, house renovator, village postman, sailboat-delivery cook/crewman, EFL teacher, and warden of backpackers' hostels in Ireland.

TALES FOR MY DOG

David Heidenstam

Grey Dolphin Press

Cover design: Emir Orucevic (Pulp.Art)
Theatrical masks artwork: Elizabeth Aragon

Set in Garamond Nova Pro by Grey Dolphin Press
Main cover typeface: Gilligans Island Regular

Grey Dolphin Press logo typeface:
Champagne and Limousines © Lauren Thompson
www.nymphont.com

ISBN: 978-0-9955934-0-4 (pbk.)
A CIP catalogue record for this book is available from
the British Library.

First edition
2022 2021 2020 2019 2018   1 2 3 4 5 6 7 8 9 10

Printed in Poland by booksfactory.co.uk

Published by Grey Dolphin Press, 2018.
www.greydolphinpress.com   admin@greydolphinpress.com
11 Temple Close, Barnwood, Gloucester, GL4 3ER, U.K.

For H
who deserved better

and even now I must ask her
to share this dedication with
my father
FH (1918–2011)
the first reader of many of these stories.

Contents

To the reader.....xi

Part One

Being famous.....3
Walking.....4
The person.....5
Leaving.....6
Learning the language.....7
The secret.....8
Freedom.....9
The liar.....10
Getting it right.....11
Making the omelette.....13
The blue jacket.....14
The misunderstanding.....15
The heart.....16
The miser.....17
The student of greatness.....19
The wish.....20
Married life.....21
Keeping a dog.....23
How art began.....24
The aesthetic life.....26
The end.....27

Cultural exchanges.....29

The film.....30

The song.....32

The chance.....33

How things became ordinary.....34

On not feeling guilty.....35

The real thing.....36

On the beach.....37

The three of them.....38

Harvest home.....39

Evening shift.....40

Under the skin.....41

Winning hearts.....42

Bargain.....43

Whole earth catalogue.....45

The ruler of the land.....46

Forgetting.....47

The job.....48

Life is a two-headed god.....50

The lost master.....51

Interlude: Four tales for younger dogs

The pig pen.....55

The thinker.....56

How to change your name.....58

The three gates.....59

Part Two

On the heath.....63

Being civilised.....64

The revenge.....66

The wedding.....68

The journey.....69

The letter.....71

The accident.....73

The paper dragons.....74

On the road.....78

The gift.....80

Being young somewhere.....81

In the bar.....83

The exile.....84

Other lives.....85

How it is.....87

The hook of the sea.....88

How to kill a chicken.....90

Waiting.....91

The parents of the nightmare.....93

Lying in the sun.....94

The woman in white.....95

Heartland.....96

The silence.....97

Back of beyond.....99

The stalker.....100

The accursed.....102
The forger.....103
The archipelago of the dead.....104
The wide world.....106
The creation myth of the marsh people.....107
The notice.....108
The moondreamer.....109
Going hence.....110
After.....112
Happier as a dog.....114

*

Notes & acknowledgements.....116
Thanks, disclaimer, gratitude.....118

* * *

To the reader

With stories this short,
it's tempting to browse, dip in.
Well – it's in your hands!
But if you do, you may lose something.

*

Some of these stories use
inverted commas for speech, some don't.
Please don't blame editors.
This kind of thing drives them crazy too.

* *

Part One

Being famous

He was a famous man. He wasn't sure what he was famous for, he couldn't really remember. But he did know he was famous. Everyone came up to him and said, It's you, isn't it; and he agreed it was. And they asked him for his signature, they gave him something to sign, a scrap of paper or a book or a photograph, and sometimes, if it was a woman, even an item of underwear. And he signed them, and smiled, and they thanked him, and shook his hand if they were forward enough, and everyone was happy. Sometimes he heard them say – You know, he's just like his photographs; which did seem likely. And sometimes he heard them say – He's still himself, isn't he; and that seemed possible too. And he was happy that he was famous. And he was happy that it made people happy to meet him. And he wondered if he would be even happier if he knew why he was famous, if he could remember. And he decided no, it didn't matter, it might be something important, it might be something stupid. But since everyone else was satisfied with the present arrangement, well then he guessed he was too.

Walking

The child walked alongside the railway track carrying a suitcase tied up with string. Inside the suitcase were clothes, and some papers he was supposed to show people. Inside the child's head were words. The child walked in a straight line, alongside the straight track. The words went round in his head. This annoyed him. He thought, if he could make his body go in a straight line, why couldn't he do the same with his head? He was young, and it was the first time that he had watched his own mind while it made him unhappy, going round and round words. Later he would know that the words were not like a track, they were like the wheels of a train. They would go round and round, but the train would go somewhere, and when the words stopped turning you would be somewhere else, and get off, and leave the words behind you. You just had to wait till that happened, and you couldn't know how long it would take. So later, he would know this. But this was the first time he'd watched his mind, hurting him; so now all he could do was walk on straight, not knowing that anything would ever change.

The person

I'd often seen him walking along the street or sitting in a café. He wasn't someone I said hello to, or nodded to, or thought about. Until one day someone leant over to me and said – You know, he's the one who... So then of course I looked at him quite differently. He still looked ordinary. I mean, if you hadn't known, you wouldn't have been able to tell. But once you knew, you could see it. Something in the eyes, or the mouth, or the lines around the nose. I was glad when I'd worked it out. So one day I leant across to someone I knew a little, and said, You can see it in his eyes, that he was the one who... And the other person looked at me and said, Who? And I nodded. And he said, No, no, you're wrong, whoever told you that? It wasn't him at all. In fact, I always understood it was you. And he went back to his newspaper. Soon after that I stopped going to cafés, or anywhere very much. There are too many people in this world, and you can't tell anything about their lives.

Leaving

Leaving's hard, they say. Or easy, of course. Depending. Anyway, I left. It was snowing. And raining of course. Possibly at the same time. Certainly alternately. And at the same time, of course, I was arriving. That being a necessary condition of movement. (Please consult a geometry or geography teacher, or a qualified driving instructor, if you have problems with this.) And naturally, since I was arriving, the sun was shining, and bands were playing, and dogs were barking, and everyone was shaking my hand. I kept on moving though. It would have been good to stop, if only as a gesture of meteorological responsibility. But I'd become rather accustomed to the leaving. Being hard. Or easy. Depending.

Learning the language

The other person in the room was snoring. She lay awake listening to it, as she had lain awake for many years, trying to understand what it said. When she was young, it had said: You've made a mistake, you've made a mistake, you've made a mistake. It said, you cannot love me, because after all I am not loveable. And what is the point of being young, if after all you cannot love? Then, when she was older, it had said: You might have done worse, you might have done worse, you might have done worse. It said, you cannot despise me, because after all you chose me. And what was the point of choosing, if you were not making a choice? And now she was old, it said: You cannot regret me, you cannot regret me, you cannot regret me. It said, make anything different, you make everything different; and then what was the meaning of your life? And that was the language, as she chose to learn it. Though she understood, very well, if she had listened differently, she might have heard differently; and then everything else too might have changed.

The secret

I'm not going to tell you the secret, she said.

He'd already shown her his badge. You have to, he said.

No, she said.

So he told her that very bad things would happen, if she didn't tell him. They would happen to her, and her family, and the country, and maybe even to God.

So in the end she told him.

And that is the secret? he said.

That was the secret, she said.

Her pedantry failed to please him.

That wasn't worth being a secret, he said.

I'm sorry, she said. But only I knew it. And it was the only thing only I knew that I knew.

He stood quietly and thought, and she stood quietly too.

So that's how you do it? he said.

Yes, she said. If you don't want it to stick to the bottom of the pan.

O.k., he said.

So will anything very bad happen to me, she asked, or my family, or the country, or maybe even to God?

No, he said. No. Well, nothing new.

Freedom

The pen ended up on the planet of lost pens. Which – as others have reported – is where all pens go, once they've vanished down the black holes of pockets, bags, drawers. And they should be happy. They have the company of their kind. They are not misused as oral stimuli, or door wedges, or ear cleaners, or to retrieve things that have dropped down a gap in the floorboards. If they are young, they have a stock of ink; if old, a stock of memories. I worked with the CIA, one might say. Or: you remember the Bible? – that was me. They can spend their days in doodling or calligraphy; many attend creative writing classes. And yet one senses a deep dissatisfaction. Those among them of libertarian bent argue this shows their addiction to servitude. Others, that service is the only purpose and satisfaction of life. Meanwhile, obsessive self-clicking of mechanisms is commonplace – though moralists of course say this should only occur between consenting ballpoints, in the context of a committed relationship.

The liar

I was very disappointed, when I found out I'd been lying to myself. "How could you?" I said. "Don't you value this relationship?" I hung my head. There were really no excuses. It had just taken over gradually, it had been easier that way. "Don't look like that," I said, "now you're trying to make me feel guilty." And that was true too. So then I tried to remember how it had been before. There must have been a time sometime, when I'd just looked at things the way they were; they didn't hurt so much. It must have been like that, and you'd think it would stay with you. But I couldn't remember it at all.

Getting it right

That night, for homework, we had to read the chapter on reproduction.

Next morning we were all a bit quiet. But in the end Fred spoke up. He usually did.

If I've got this right, he said, we have to swim back up the river we were born in. And swim up all the waterfalls, right to the top. And then we do it. And then afterwards we die of exhaustion.

There was a bit of a silence. Fred was our leader, and nobody wanted to contradict him. But eventually Bert spoke up.

Well, I don't know, he said. The bit I read said you had to go up in an aeroplane with the Queen.

We all cheered up. That sounded a bit better.

Only, he said, it goes higher and higher, till there's only one of you left. I don't know why. And then, when you do it, you lose your tummy.

Jim said he could believe that, because they'd flown to Spain on holiday, and he'd had to use the sickbag all the way.

Did it say what sort of aeroplane? Tom asked.

Bert said no, only he knew sometimes the royal family used helicopters to go to places.

There was a bit of a discussion about whether the Queen would be happy to do it in a helicopter or not.

Anyway, Jim said, the bit I read said you had to take

food along, as a present. Otherwise you might get eaten instead.

Fred said that sounded likely, as his big sister was always getting boxes of chocolates, and as far as he knew all her boyfriends were still alive.

Yes, Bert said, and I remember when my brother was going in the navy. I heard my Dad talking to him about foreign girls, and how he should always wear protection.

We all nodded at that. That would be if the box of chocolates isn't big enough, Jim said.

Making the omelette

The president was making the omelette. He had been appointed president by the universal acclamation of five generals, two admirals, the marshal of the airforce, and the chief of police, and he had accepted their mandate with pride. So now he was making the omelette – and he knew the ingredients well, he had studied all the recipes. There was the milk of human kindness, of course: those little reminders of past friendship or future well-being. That helped settle the stomach of the judiciary, and the still larger stomachs of the church. Then there was the salt and pepper of formality: a little savoury lawmaking, to help journalists overcome their inquisitiveness, workers their indolence, intellectuals their ignorance, and politicians their pride. But most of all, of course, there were the eggs – so many eggs to make this great omelette of a nation. Beginning with easing them from their shells, those brittle little skins of selfishness. And then – and he rolled his sleeves afresh for the work – the beating, the beating, the beating.

The blue jacket

Everybody knew about the blue jacket. You put it on, and it told you what you wanted to know. Or at least, what you thought you wanted to know. Because sometimes, once you knew, you realised you hadn't wanted to know that at all. Will my son make a success of his life? you might ask. Of course, the jacket might say; everyone will respect him for inheriting so much money so young. Or: Does my wife really love me? – No, but then she doesn't love any of her other lovers either. Or: Will I be famous? – Oh yes – (it might say) – as will everyone caught up in that unpleasant business. It certainly had a sardonic sense of the world, that blue jacket. Of course, its replies were, by their nature, somewhat difficult for the listener to verify. So whether it was also honest, that blue jacket – or had merely learnt, from too much hanging around on humans, the pleasures of telling people what they don't know and don't want to – no human, and possibly no other item of clothing, could absolutely say.

The misunderstanding

I had a misunderstanding the other day. I thought I was a pastry cook, but then realised I was Chief of Police. My colleagues were looking at me strangely. It's nothing, I said, it's just a misunderstanding. Eventually they left me to myself, and life got back to usual. Only sometimes, in the middle of an interrogation, I'll realise I've been explaining the difference between filo and choux, or the best way to make Apfelstrudel. And then I'll scowl, and hit the table, and tell the prisoner he had better confess quickly. Or else I'll tell him what they do to pastry in Russia; and *then* he'll wish he'd never been born.

The heart

You've stolen my heart, he said.

Which was true.

She'd approached three fences well known to the police, but they'd refused to touch it.

She'd had it analysed to see if its elements were valuable, and been entirely disappointed.

She'd tried to use it as deposit for a mortgage on a one-bedroom apartment, but the rate of interest they wanted was just outrageous.

She'd taken it to a pawnshop, and been laughed out of the place.

She'd offered it to a transplant hospital, but had it returned as not matching any foreseeable requirements.

She'd tried to use it as petfood, but her cat preferred canned rabbit chunks in gravy.

She'd even asked about donating it to a museum, but been told that no-one wanted to look at that sort of thing any more.

So she sent it back. Only to have it returned, marked, "No longer wanted on voyage."

The miser

He was a miser, and so didn't buy any clothes. Sometimes someone from out of town would stop and point and want to call the police. But then people would reassure them, and smile, and shake their heads, and say, no, no, it's all right, it's only the miser. And a few even envied him, because they thought it must be quite practical not to have to get your clothes laundered all the time – especially if you were a miser, because then you wouldn't have to pay anyone else to do it. But most people were very glad they had their clothes, because they felt that with clothes they could deceive people into loving them. The miser, of course, didn't care about anyone loving him, since he had a different love, which was far more dependable. Fortunately he was wealthy. It is, I suppose, possible to imagine a poor miser, though it feels like an insult to the realities of poverty. But he was a wealthy miser, and he loved his wealth like a true lover, with all his heart and all his attention. He wanted to buy it presents, and make it look beautiful, and keep it warm and happy. And if others thought it inanimate and incapable of reciprocating, that of course was just their stupidity. For all the time his wealth filled his life with infinite dreams of possibility. He could, he knew, use it to travel to the moon, or build hospitals, or start a war, or find a beautiful wife. And one day he might do these things – use it selfishly or wisely or terribly, or in a futile assault on someone's heart. But in the meantime, he waited, studying the world, and his own nature, and what might bring him most happiness. And gradually he was concluding, that none of these realities could ever satisfy him. For he was already as happy as he ever could be, living without clothes and with infinite dreams.

The student of greatness

So he broke into the warehouse and stole forty police jackets.

They were pretty good, almost coats really, with fur-lined collars, and a badge at the top of each sleeve, a round patch with a shield and the word "police" underneath.

He showed them to his friend.

"Great gear, eh?" he said.

His friend looked at them. "Yes," he said. "Er – what were you going to do with them?"

"Well, I thought, the Sunday market."

His friend looked at him in a certain way.

Our hero had not made an unnecessary habit of reading. But – if asked – he would have said that true greatness lay not only in being extremely quick on the uptake, but also decisive in action.

"I know," he said. "I'll take them back."

His friend looked at him.

"You'll take them back," he said.

"Yes," he said. "I mean, people do it all the time. The colour looks different when they get it in the light; or the style's wrong; or the wife doesn't like it."

And that is why it is still remembered, in our town; that when the police station changed shifts early on Monday morning, they found forty items of uniform on the pavement outside; piled neatly; all in their original wrappers; and a note attached on top, saying – "Sorry, wrong size."

The wish

He made a wish. That didn't do any good. So he got a haircut, bought new clothes and sunglasses, and started keep-fit classes. No dice. Took up art and claimed to be writing a novel. Nothing. Went into politics. Oh no. Joined the security services, went round with half a dozen body-guards, and tortured people enthusiastically. Better, but he doubted the sincerity of the protestations. Plotted a coup, overthrew the government, made himself president for life, declared war on everyone, and conquered several continents. Ah, finally, that did it. No doubting the genuineness of the admiration and love. All you have to do is persevere.

Married life

How it happened was, he went down to the shops to get a few things, and who should he bump into but this guy he knew from way back. So they laughed, and got talking, and then they stopped in a pub to relax and talk some more, and the next thing they knew it was getting late and they were getting hungry, so they went to this food place and had the curry and chips, and then they felt a bit thirsty again, and so they went into another pub and had a few more drinks. And somewhere along the line, somewhere in all that, the shopping must have got put down and left behind – in the first pub probably, only he wasn't sure which pub that was, and anyway he only realised when he got home and you were waiting thinking he'd been hit by a lorry or something and he didn't have the bread or the nappies or the milk or any of the stuff. So you're pretty pissed off, but you know he's got to have his own space, so you keep it cool and say, Ok, well, who was this guy, what's his name? So that's when he says, Well, actually, I couldn't exactly remember, and after we'd gone through all the hellos and the backslapping I couldn't very well ask – so he'd gone through the whole evening not being able to say this guy's name. And now he comes to think about it, he says, I can't remember him using *my* name either – so maybe the other guy couldn't quite remember his name, just the same. And then he's a bit quiet for a bit and thinks some more. And then he says, in fact, now he *really* thinks about it, he wasn't *absolutely* sure that the guy had actually been who he'd thought he was at the beginning. But what the hell; it had been really great seeing someone again all the same.

Keeping a dog

Having a dog is quite a business, let me tell you.

It needs to be fed, it needs to be walked, it needs to have a life it can live. You can't just let it die of boredom.

They try to fit in with you, of course. Take an interest.

But there's a limit to it. They start yawning. They don't have the concentration we do. Not for our things anyway. Why should they?

Easier to keep a mistress really. They have to be fed, and walked too if possible, but only occasionally, not every day. And they try to take an interest, and yawn, and don't really have the concentration, not for your things anyway, why should they? But you know they've got plenty of other lives they don't tell you about, so you don't feel guilty about it. Not like you would if they were a dog.

How art began

Each year the villagers put a sacrifice out. A maiden or a bullock or several fine goats. And for generations, they were dealt with satisfactorily. There might be suitable sounds in the night – a shriek, a bleat, a struggle. And in the morning the clearing would be empty again, just some battered vegetation and an appropriate amount of blood.

But then gradually their deity's appetite seemed to diminish. A leg might be left, or one goat, or even a buttock or two. The villagers tried to present the sacrifices more temptingly, using expensive spices and marinades, so far as their isolation, the ecclesiastical budget, and the mobile nature of the cuisine allowed. But still the decline in consumption continued, until one morning the intended sacrifice was found alive and untouched. Being a young woman called Ursula, it was articulately indignant in its disappointment, complaining that they couldn't have dressed her finely or skimpily enough. They put her out again the following night, in very limited apparel of her own devising, but to no avail. In a fit of pique, she applied to marry herself off into another village; and through embarrassment at her presence, and uncertainty about the social and spiritual status of unclaimed sacrifices, this irregularity went unopposed.

After that, the villagers devoted ever more time and resources to preparing each year's intended sacrifice; but their efforts were unrewarded. They argued over whether the deity had died, or grown old, or just wandered away. In fact, now there was, in truth, no sacrifice, they began to argue about many things. But this was also when a great lassitude came over the people. For if even a god can lose its most bestial appetites, what hope is there for human lusts? A few of the most despondent began to paint, or create music, or write short stories – perversions of a creative impulse that had previously inspired cooking, hairdressing, and couture. But even such degenerates could not suppose, that this was any substitute for what had been lost.

The aesthetic life

The punk time-travel collective aimed to destroy as much of the present as possible. Not – their manifesto stressed – for any political purpose. It was simply a high form of conceptual art. Of course, usually their retrospective interference also succeeded in effacing their own existence. So then someone had to come up with the idea all over again. Eventually their most brilliant practitioner succeeded in going back and erasing the entire universe. There was, of course, no-one around to appreciate this achievement – but that didn't matter. It was well known that the true artist should be utterly selfless and selfish, in their dedication to their art.

The end

It was the end. The horse had ridden away into the sunset, with a hero on board. A heroine had watched him go, cradling in her arms her crippled husband whom she'd never loved. The ranch was burnt and smoking, but the Indians had been beaten off. The villains were all dead. The cattle were safe. The crops were in. The sheriff was alive, and life had taught a lesson to his cold-hearted bride. The Mexicans were in retreat. The townspeople were free from fear. The farmer had paid off his mortgage. The girl had been rescued from the railway track. The oil barons had been broken. The honest man had made president. The mobsters were all in jail. The workers were all working. Everyone had got to California. The starlet had found stardom. A tiny but strategically important Pacific island had been recaptured, though many brave men were dead. The altitude record had been broken. The newly-wed was deliriously happy with her cooker, vacuum cleaner, and washing machine. The young were full of fun but respectful. The swingers had all found that it's love that really matters. Though they might never be the same, the draftees had come back from Vietnam. Honour had been restored at the heart of government. Wealth had trickled down to the destitute. The spacemen had been rescued from the capsule. Misguided foreigners had been taught all kinds of lessons. And, as usual, the monster from the deep – or the past, or the stars – had died in agony; though there was just a hint that maybe its eggs still lay fertile somewhere, ready to hatch just in time for a sequel in a year or so.

Cultural exchanges

We gave them cricket. They gave us Michelangelo, Rembrandt, and van Gogh. We gave them football. They gave us Mozart, Beethoven, Verdi, and Janis Joplin. We gave them darts. They gave us Plato and Aristotle. We gave them snooker. They gave us Balzac, Tolstoy, Dostoevsky and Proust. We gave them tennis and badminton. They gave us the Taj Mahal. We gave them golf. They gave us the Bible, the Talmud, the Bhagavad Gita and the Koran. I mean – Well – How bloody ungrateful can you get..??

The film

He had money. A lot of money.

I want to make a film, he said.

Fine, they said.

I want this misunderstood man, he said. He's the hero.

We can all relate to that, they said.

And he loves his wife, but she thinks he doesn't. And he's the one who really makes things work at work, only they all think he's useless. And there's going to be a catastrophe, and he tries to warn people, but no-one listens. And he discovers there's been this great injustice done, only something happens, so it looks like he's got it all wrong. And then there's this mistaken identity, and he gets charged with fraud – so even his family don't trust him any more.

So far so good, they said.

And so his wife divorces him. He loses his job – someone else gets all the credit, and he gets the blame for all the mistakes. The catastrophe happens, but nobody remembers what he said. The great injustice never gets uncovered. And he's convicted of the fraud, and even his lawyers think he's guilty. And when he finally gets released, he dies penniless and alone, and nobody even mentions his name. And that's how it ends, he said.

Bearing in mind his money, they thought about this for five seconds.

Why do you want to make this film? they said.

Because I want one film, he said – just one – one book or story or poem or play or film – in the history of the world, he said – that actually told the truth.

You're sick, they said.

The song

The singer was singing about love, death, hope, despair. The song was a long one. In fact, while it went on, people loved, and died, and hoped, and despaired, and so there was always something new to sing about. Indeed the song had been going on for as long as anyone could say, though only fools and madmen ever thought they'd seen the singer. But the singer, even so, didn't seem to be getting at all tired. So it was best to assume that it was going to go on being sung for quite a good while yet.

The chance

It was a fifty-fifty chance. Either the ball would land on the right number, and he'd win, and he'd put it all on the same number again, and that would come up too, and he'd be able to pay off what was missing, and they wouldn't have noticed yet, and he'd get away, and find his girl again, and she'd realise she'd made a mistake, and he'd get a farm somehow, and they'd have kids, and the crops would come up, and the weather hold, and the prices, and nobody would come after him, and no-one would ever know, and he'd nod to the neighbours, and sit in his slippers, and go to church on Sundays. Or maybe not. It was a fifty-fifty chance, he thought. You couldn't ask fairer than that.

How things became ordinary

Him

They were getting on well. She liked the same movies as he did, and the same music, and the same way of making love. And they occupied the same space without problem, they didn't grate or jar on each other, they were at ease. And so they moved in together and gradually they began to take on the roles, you know, they were a couple. And things weren't always perfect of course, not even ever perfect; because what is 'perfect', how do you know perfect?, that's not a human judgement, that's a judgement for gods. But they were good, and honest, and easy, and that was all there was, he thought; that was all there could ever be.

Her

He pretended he didn't care. "It's ok," he said.

She knew it wasn't so, but what could she say?

"Ok," she said. She didn't want to make a thing of it.

So they went through the day, and that evening they quarrelled. It wasn't a big quarrel, or at least it was a quiet one; and they made up afterwards. But it didn't really feel like they'd made up.

And that, for her, was how they settled down, and ordinary life began for them. As if there'd been a lion sitting there, with one paw on each of them. And the lion had got up and walked away.

On not feeling guilty

Many people went to the war, and many didn't come back. He was one who did, and didn't feel guilty about that at all. He didn't know if it was luck, or something else – he thought it was just luck. But whatever it was, he wasn't going to feel guilty about it. And he didn't feel guilty about getting the girl of someone who didn't come back, and marrying her, and having kids, and being happy. And he worked hard, till he could set up on his own, and then he worked even harder and did well. And whatever it was that had been with him, stayed with him, the luck or whatever. And he didn't even think much about the past, or about the ones who hadn't come back. But when he did, it was with a kind of gratitude. Because going to the war and coming back, that had given his life a meaning, that it couldn't ever lose. And it couldn't have had that meaning, without them going and not coming back.

The real thing

The old man sat in the beach café, dressed in the special clothes he'd brought with him: the leather boots, and the parti-coloured jodhpurs with buckles all down the legs, and the bright belt and braces, and the broad felt hat. He seemed strange among the other tourists, in their sunbathing clothes, or their travellers' trousers covered in pockets, or their silk scarves against the sun. But this was still his holiday each year, to come back to this land, where he had once fought for a beaten army; and ride on the beach, and sit quietly in the café in between. And off to one side a little way the horse he rode was standing waiting, hitched loosely to a pole, a bucket of water on the ground near his head. There was a breeze, and no flies, so the horse did not even flick his tail, just stood four-square drooping a bit. The two-leg knew how to sit on a horse, thought the horse; knew how to be still and how not to be still. Better than a dead weight, or gripping too tight, or children's feet kicking your side. And the man too knew that he knew how to ride. And the horse knew, too, that the clothes were part of that. And it was good to be on the beach, thought the man, thought the horse. But it wasn't the same as being young.

On the beach

There were two of them. One fat, one thin. One old, one young. One rich, one poor. One greedy, one needy.

He watched her for a long time before speaking. There was no need to speak, because being on a beach with many others made silence natural. And it was easy to watch, because being on a beach with many others, and the glare of the sun, and the concealment of sunglasses, made glances easy, ambiguous, innocuous.

Or they might have been innocuous, if she had not been so aware of them.

And eventually he spoke, and she knew she had to decide. And it was like she was watching a film or reading a book, and there's that sickness in your stomach, because you are watching everything go wrong. You can see it coming, the thing that will change everything, that will mark everything for ever. The action, the decision, the choice. And you know there is nothing you can do to stop the film or change the story. Because, however much you might wish you could change it, it will always be the wrong choice that will be made.

Only, she noticed, when it's your own life, not a story, you don't actually feel it so much.

The three of them

The three of them were back together again. It was a long time since they'd tried to pull off a job, and never one as big as this. Well, the past was the past; no point in looking back; no time now for worries or regrets. He interlocked his hands, flexed his fingers, nodded to the others. Ready? Yes. This was it. There was going to be an almighty bang. But this time, this time it was going to work. They knew the script, knew their jobs. There was nothing to go wrong. Creation, Redemption, and the gift of Grace. Father, Son, and Holy Ghost.

Harvest home

Suddenly one Sunday he went insane.

I'm going to give you a haircut, he said. I'm going to give you a haircut.

He caught his wife and was about to slit her throat when his son got him over the head with an iron pan.

They tied his feet and hands while he was out, then called the constabulary. When they came, he was jolting on his back almost like he had the water fear. But it wasn't that. There'd been no mad animals; only him.

When he'd gone, the wife crouched in a corner, shaking and weeping. The son held her shoulder and thought of his inheritance: debt, dead cattle, dead land.

Too dumb to just top himself, was what was said after. And of course they all said they'd seen it coming a long time.

Evening shift

The fan was going round erratically, sometimes clickety clacking, sometimes clackety clicking. Underneath the fan, three men were crowded into the small room. Two of them were standing up, holding batons in their hands, and not screaming. After a while the screaming stopped, which took the fun out of things. So the standing men gave a couple of final kicks, and turned away, and went out the door, and a little later the other one stopped breathing and started rotting. Later still someone looked in, saw the body, checked for a pulse, and switched off the fan.

Under the skin

He made a journey, to go to those places where so many
people had been killed. Not his people mostly, but it was in
the world's memory now, he'd known the names since
childhood. Though he knew there were other places too,
nameless, where people had been brought and made to dig
their own graves. He queued, and looked, and read, and
bowed his head in silence. And one evening he took a
sleeper train, across the borderlands of eastern Europe. Late
into the night, he felt the train stop; then, after a time,
strangely, it began to run back for a while, and then stop
again. To do with changing the gauge, perhaps? He knew
they had to change gauge in the night. He rolled over in the
bunk, and lifted the edge of the curtain – and felt a strange
stab of fear. Just an innocent train; stopped, in the middle of
the night, in a clearing in a dark forest. But now, at last, his
mind could stand inside the nightmare.

Winning hearts

He wasn't sure, but they looked like bad guys, so he shot them anyway. Then he saw some more, and shot them as well. For a moment he wondered if he was doing the right thing. But then he thought of what they might have done if they'd been bad guys, if he hadn't shot them. This made him mad. It always made him mad when you tried to help people, and you ended up having to kill them instead. People like that had no decency, no appreciation, no human feelings. It almost made you wish you hadn't got started on all of this. And then where would we be?

Bargain

Ah, but you should have seen him when he was young. Now there was a god for you. Of course, he was only a local god when he started out. Lot of competition. You don't know what it was like back then. I mean, humanity had been around for a while, but they'd only just got around to *thinking* about things. It was god against god out there, and you couldn't be too squeamish. He was pretty clued up though, stuck to what he was good at – did the war god thing a lot, and the burnt offering thing. Didn't bother with the temple oracle routine or the ritual sex thing; concentrated more on killing off the opposition than mass appeal. When it came to broadening out a bit, adding a bit more morality, a bit more style, he let the humans do it for him. Let the scribes and the prophets work it all out for themselves. Not that they ever agreed with each other, but no-one worried too much about that. And then when the time came, you have to give it to him. No idea who thought it up. Might even have been him, it was crazy enough. But respect and that, he picked it up and ran with it. And you can imagine the commotion. I mean, he goes along to the council, tells all the other gods he's got an announcement, tells them he's going to do a human incarnation as his own son, and he's going to get himself bumped off in some really nasty way, and *that's* going to pay for all the sins of mankind! I mean – talk about one-upmanship – talk about chutzpah. Half the gods were rolling around on the floor, they couldn't stop laughing, they were pissing themselves, the other half were just sitting there with their jaws dropped through their boots. I mean – what? how? whoa.. – it didn't make any *sense*! All right, go down, share the lifestyle, feel the pain – all very commendable. Hardly original; but worthy enough. But redeeming humanity? past, present, and future?? everything *that lot* manage to get up to??? just because you've let an incarnation of yourself be strung up on trumped-up charges???? It didn't figure, it didn't compute. God, he had balls, though. Stuck to his guns. You've got to remember, this was the Middle East. Start out asking for a hundred shekels and be happy with twenty. That's what everyone thought – he'd come down, haggle a bit, already had a nice little compromise in mind, something everyone could live with. No way. This was it. No bazaar here, this was a fixed price deal. Still don't know how he got it through. Not sure if *he* did! Lot of politicking by his gang, lots of debts called in, lots of IOUs for the future. But that was how it happened. Don't know if he really worked out the implications, though. I mean, you're dealing with humanity, okay? *Homo sapiens sapiens*. Sharp as razors and thick as pigshit. Once *they* get ideas in their heads, it can *really* screw things up.

Whole earth catalogue

All over the world, people were dying of ignorance. But mostly it was other people's ignorance they were dying of, so there wasn't much they could do about it.

The ruler of the land

A long time ago – before even your father was born – there was a great debate among the animals, over who should rule the land. The eagle ruled the sky, and no-one could rule the sea; but no-one knew who would rule the land. The cleverest animal was the monkey, but he was also the most foolish; so the others would not submit to see him rule. The wisest animal was the elephant, but he was too wise to do it – especially since he thought no other animal could rule him. The fiercest animal was the lion, and no-one could defeat him. But it was no good to have a ruler who slept his days away in the sun. The deadliest was the snake, but he was also the most hated. The others only wanted to see his spine crushed in the sand. The fox and goat were cunning, but neither had the cunning of a ruler. The sheep and the deer were peaceful – but much too shy to try to rule. So the land came to be ruled by the creature they all feared but could not vanquish. Who crawled from out of crevices, and stalked into their dreams. They would not do him homage; but to him that did no matter. And that – my proud ones! – is how the land, became the realm of the scorpion king.

Forgetting

The food was delicious. It was boiled turnip and old bread without butter and dry peas and the carcass of a chicken from three days ago. When you couldn't eat any more, you asked if you could take some of it away with you in a bag. But they laughed and said no, and told you to come back tomorrow, when it would be even older. So you did, came back the next day, and the food wasn't so delicious this time. So they sent you away again, and you came back each day, till the food tasted dry and bland and stale and old. And then they said that was it, you'd passed the test, it was o.k., you could be a human being. You didn't have to be a god any more.

The job

It was a tough assignment, and you didn't have much time. First you had to get out of bed. Then you had to make some coffee, and drink it, and wash and shave, and get your clothes on, and catch the bus, and get to work, and get everything done, and go out and get to the bank at lunchtime, and the drycleaners too if possible. And then get through the afternoon, and then of course in the evening come home, and wash, and feed, and wash the dishes, and watch the evening news, and a bit of whatever was on, and then get to bed and maybe get a good night's sleep. And the same tomorrow. And then of course you had to pay the bills sometime; and go back and see your parents. And try to decide about the woman you were seeing, whether to ask if she'd marry you, you think she might say yes. And if you got married, whether you'd both want to go on working like now, or if you'd hope to have kids straightaway. And then you'd have to bring them up, and let the grandparents see them, and have family holidays. And fit in rows, and affairs, and divorce, because that was what usually happened. And voting! – you were forgetting about voting. And then the children going off, and not seeing you very much, and you retiring and maybe losing your health or your mind and eventually dying of something or other. And it was a hell of a lot, when you thought about it. You'd try of course; of course you would. You'd do your best. But you didn't really see how you were going to have the time, not really, not for all of it. You didn't see how they could expect you to fit it all in.

Life is a two-headed god

Nothing mattered if you were sitting in the sunshine. That was what he decided. Everything could be wrong, but if you were sitting in the sunshine and you had a coffee in front of you, and the money for it, then nothing could really be very wrong. And he thought about his wife and his job and his house and his boss, and he looked out over the water in the sunshine, and sipped his coffee, and listened to others chattering around him, and sat and breathed and breathed.

The couple at the next table were embarrassed by this stranger, who sat with tears running down his face.

The woman found a tissue and held it out to him.

Here, she said, you could dry your eyes with that.

He looked at her.

Why would I want to do that? he said.

The lost master

This is a story about a reward. You see, this dog lost its master. So it put up notices all around town – on lampposts, and in cafés, and even in the lost and found column of the newspaper. You know the kind of thing, you see them all the time. "Lost, one human being. Short coat, brown. Friendly nature. Answers to the name of Roy." Anyway, at first there was no news, nothing at all. But the dog persevered, because it had been quite fond of its master, and didn't like to think of it wandering around out there with no-one to bring it its slippers or its newspaper, or to take it for a walk in the evening, or to bring back all the sticks it liked to throw. So the dog put up more notices, and put Reward in big letters. And eventually, sure enough, his master turned up again, as if nothing had happened, only looked a bit sheepish and snuffled a bit. Human beings lack the gift of faithfulness, of course; with them it is merely a virtue. But they can make quite good masters, and sometimes they come back. And maybe sometimes it helps if they know their dog has cared enough to even offer a reward.

* *

Interlude

Four tales for younger dogs

The pig pen
(for very young dogs)

You think you know what a pig pen is. It's a little house for a pig. Or piglets. In a field or a farmyard. Only this wasn't that sort of pig pen. This pig pen was for writing with. It made the writing difficult, of course. It was hard to hold, and heavy, and wriggly. So if you started writing an A, you might end up with an E. Or if you started writing your name, you might end up with a recipe for chocolate ice cream. And it squealed of course. And ate all the time. Which made the paper messy. And its feet might hit you in the eye. But it was the only pen you had, the pig pen. So you kept on writing with it; you kept on trying. Because you wanted to write, and you knew it was supposed to be difficult. But you knew it would only get easier if you really really tried.

The thinker
(for not quite so young young dogs)

He had been listening to the grownups, which seemed to be a dangerous thing to do. Because his mother had said, "So-and-so doesn't know which side his bread is buttered." And she'd laughed. And that was several days ago. And now he lay awake, and he was very worried. He could ask, of course. But he wanted to solve this himself, it seemed very important to do that. Because – which side is your bread buttered? Of course, once it's buttered, that's the side it's buttered – anyone can see that. But how do you tell beforehand? He had looked at slices of bread, lots of them, and there was no sign on them, saying "Please butter this side." It would be very helpful, but there wasn't. He supposed maybe it was to do with the expense, or perhaps the difficulty of printing on bread. And he had looked very carefully, and he could see no difference between the two sides of a slice of bread – whether it was ready cut or one you cut yourself. They both seemed very much the same. Of course, at the ends you could tell, because one side was hard, and you definitely didn't butter that one. And of course you could use that as a guide, as you worked inwards. But then at the other end there was a piece facing the other way, which would tell you the opposite. Unless you were supposed to work in to the middle from one end, and then in to the middle from the other – but he'd never seen a grownup do that. And anyway, how would you remember where the middle was, when the ends weren't there any more? So then he wondered if there was something printed on the package. Like with paper for computers. They had an arrow on the end, to tell you which way up to put them. Only, he wasn't sure if that worked very well, because he'd seen his father scratch his head, and try turning the paper one way or another, and look at it carefully, as if he wasn't sure if the arrow was supposed to go up or down. And anyway, he'd looked at packets of bread, and there weren't any arrows on them. And some bread didn't even come in packets. So finally he'd watched them, the grownups, buttering the bread. And he couldn't see how they did it. They just seemed to take the piece of bread and know straightaway. So maybe that was the point. That it was a grownup thing. Something you learnt. But he wasn't sure about that either, because he'd seen his sister buttering bread, and she was only a bit older and didn't have much trouble – anyway, not with knowing which side. And his mother never said to her, oh no, you've buttered the wrong side. So he lay in bed and worried about it, and he was sure he ought to be able to work it out by himself, which side your bread was buttered. Because it sounded as if it was important. And in the meantime, he thought maybe he wouldn't listen to what grownups said any more. At least, not until he was a grownup. Because it seemed to be a dangerous thing to do. And that was a pity. Because if he had asked his mother, she would have been able to tell him, that everything he had thought, was really very clever indeed.

How to change your name
(for a little bit older young dogs)

There was once a boy called Luke; which upset him a great deal. Because whenever something wasn't hot enough – the soup, or the bath, or the tea – his father would say, "Hey, this is only luke warm." Which made him realise that a luke something wasn't a proper something. If something was hot it was hot, and if it was cold it was cold; but if it was luke, it was only second best. And he wondered if other things could be luke. Is it a really scary story? – No, it's only sort of luke scary. Is your sister nice to you? – Well, sometimes she's almost luke nice. And in church, on Sunday, they sometimes read from something called Luke. And Luke sounded pretty luke. Some things they read out were quite good, with trumpets and battles and plagues; they weren't luke at all. But Luke was really just luke. And so he wondered what he should do. He had another name, which was Benjamin. And no-one said, it's only benjamin warm. Or even, it's only ben warm, for short. He'd heard his mother say, "Oh, it's been warm." But he was sensible enough to know that that wasn't the same thing. So he thought, maybe he'd be Benjamin and not Luke. But then he thought, if you're Luke, you're Luke, you can't change things like that. And he was right and he was wrong. Because when he grew up, he did things no-one had ever done before, and became very famous. And because of what he did, everything changed, and no-one ever said "It's only luke warm" again. Instead they said, "Huh – this is only benjamin warm."

The three gates
(for almost no longer young young dogs)

On the road are three gates. And each gate has a guardian.

And to pass each gate you must ask the right question. Or the guardian will not let you go through.

The first gate, you come to when you are not yet full grown. And the question you must ask is, What shall I sing?

And the guardian at that gate is a holy man. And if at that gate you ask the wrong question, he leads you into the desert to die.

And the second gate, you come to when you are grown and out in the world. And the question you must ask is, What shall I build?

And the guardians at that gate are your father and your mother. And if at that gate you ask the wrong question, they drag you down into the swamp to rot.

And the third gate, you come to when you are getting old. And the question you must ask is, What shall I burn?

And the guardian at that gate is the whole wide world. And if at that gate you ask the wrong question, all that you lack crushes the breath out of you.

And only you can answer each question; and only after you have passed each gate.

And if you do not pass the gates, an evening may come, when all the past will taste of dust. For at each gate, you can turn aside, or go around, and so escape. Only, of course, not with your life.

* *

Part Two

Some of the stories in Part Two are true.

On the heath

On Sundays everyone walks on the heath. On the hill, they fly kites. On the playing fields, they kick balls about. Some walk with dogs, or prams, or lovers. But it's a big place, and there are deserted paths through the trees, and empty stretches between like meadows, green and quiet. Suddenly, turning a corner, you come upon a sculpture, two metres of metal, vaguely human. It's up near the great house, where people come for art exhibitions and cream teas, or sit on the grass for concerts in the summer. They must have set up an outdoor exhibition since you were here last. Further on, commanding the long open slope of a field, there's another, a huge piece in green-tinged bronze, a ton or more of metal in two separate pieces on a metre-high plinth. You go round it, peer at the inscription: "Two-piece reclining figure No. 5," it says. "Henry Moore. 1963–4." You stand there, trying to work out how the two bits fit together. Seen too close, like this, the lower limbs seem massively unrelated to the torso. Just then, two children approach, looking solemn and doubtful. Perhaps they're also having trouble putting together the two bits. Then one of them, the older, speaks, pointing to one of the two halves. "*That* one," he says decisively, "is still alive."

Being civilised

He always liked meeting Jane again. They'd never been
lovers, though they'd once been close to it. But they shared
enough to make for easy company – enough memories,
enough humour, enough understanding. She'd never married, which he attributed to intelligence on her part; and
he'd never married, which they both recognised as stupidity on his. So they met occasionally, and dissected old
friends, and new films, and then went off to sample sepa-
rately a little more of life, before meeting up yet again.
Neither of them felt any dissatisfaction with this, or any
desire to improve on it, or any sense of what improvement
there might be. So they drifted on, more or less successful
in their professions, more or less untroubled in their friendship, more or less at one with their lives.

All of which could have gone on indefinitely, if one of
them had not met someone. It doesn't matter who did the
meeting; there is no gender to this morality. Anyway, one
did – meet someone. And in due course told the other, and
arranged for them to meet. Whereupon all found themselves in a room awash with hostility; which took everyone
by surprise. It wasn't as if the lone one had come bearing a
sense of being supplanted; or as if the met one had come
with fear of what a very old friend might threaten. And yet
the feeling was there, they all recognised this. They all –
being very civilised – tried to talk about it. They knew that
their dispassion was an option of comfortable lives; but that

did not mean it was not a virtue. But it did little good, the old ease had gone. A – practical and logical – was logical and practical: if A likes B and B likes C, that's no reason why A and C should get along. B – who worked with generalities – ventured a generality: it was, perhaps, a defect of the human wit and heart, that passion and dispassion did not mix. And C? – C felt as if some ancient god had opened an eyelid and said: You can play with your lives as much as you want. But, touch the realities just once, and we will rise up – and show you how thick your blood still runs – and how very thin your reason.

The revenge

They shouldn't be trying to build a city down there. It was arid land and they were building shopping malls. People were coming in, the old town was ringed with concrete. That was what happened when you could dig money out of the ground.

It was one of the incomers who took his wife. He thought they'd been happy; happy enough. What did he know? Then one day – she was leaving him. She had a lover. An incomer with good teeth and a good job.

He just wanted to kill her, kill him. But there was no way they wouldn't catch him after. He didn't want to die too.

There was a place that he passed every day, going round, doing his job. Getting older but getting by. A construction site, started, lying idle for now; someone bankrupt or someone dead. There was just a dog guarding it, and it went mad whenever he went past, leaping at its chain, trying to get at him. Probably mad anyway, from being chained all day; he never saw anyone there. He'd have liked to have felt sorry for it, but it seemed to have a special hate for him.

He went down to the river bed where water flowed in the winter, and broke a great mound of sticks from a dead tree. He put them in a sack and took them up to where the dog was. It was Saturday, the whole area was quiet, there was nobody about.

The dog saw him – seemed surprised for a moment – seeing him out of his workday clothes. Then it started barking as usual, loud enough to wake the dead, leaping at its chain, trying to get to him. The chain held, he'd seen before how well it was fixed.

He got the sticks and he threw one of them, over the dog's head, into the bare site beyond.

The dog stopped for a moment, looking at him, looking at the stick, trying to take it in.

He threw again, then the dog went mad – running the other way, trying to get at the sticks, trying to defend its domain, running back, trying to get to him. Rearing up, as the chain caught at its throat.

He threw stick after stick, the sweat building up in his armpits, the dog slavering, running, leaping, barking, its eyes bulging, lurching full tilt at the chain.

Then suddenly it was all over. The dog dropped to the ground, its legs jerked, then it lay still. He hadn't thought it could end as well as that. He threw one more stick, but the dog just lay there. Maybe its heart had failed, maybe it had broken its neck.

The man turned his back and walked away. That was one resentment washed out of him. How often do you even get that?

The wedding

The man had met the woman through an ad. She was a foreigner and – as it turned out – looking for a husband, so that she could stay in the country. A genuine one. Not interested in anything else. Well, that ruled him out, he couldn't afford a wife, didn't particularly want one anyway. Once she realised, she made sure she got a meal out of it, instead of just the intended drink. She was very frank; had had a judge and a retired medical man interested; but only if sex was on the menu immediately, and she was too pragmatic for that. Anyway, after that, regretting his emptied wallet, he went back to an even more solitary life. But a couple of months later, got an invitation to her wedding. She'd found her husband – a small-time businessman from somewhere or other. In deference to her religion, the ceremony was in the city's appropriate cathedral. The groom's mother was there, the bride had a compatriot girl-friend as bridesmaid; the judge came along to give the bride away! A depressing affair, thought the man, feeling tired, after the reception; a few dulled people with nothing in common; himself of course included. Earlier, in the cathedral, during the ceremony, they'd held golden crowns over the bride and groom, in the tradition; and, just for a moment, you could feel the possibility of redemption, as if their vows had made them princes of the earth. Still, he knew no-one's life was likely to get touched by transcendence; or at least his wasn't. Perhaps the world was a weariness without some god or other. But that was much too reassuring to want to find one.

The journey

He had to go away, it was his job, there was no avoiding it. So for now they stood on the balcony at her place, looking out over the city. Touching arms but not looking at each other; perhaps getting used to not looking at each other.

Lights in cities at night, she thought. The one beautiful thing we've made. The one beautiful thing.

I'll write, he said. You know I'll write.

You'd bloody better, she said.

Every night, he said. An e-mail every night.

No, she said. Fuck e-mails. I want the things you can't put in e-mails. I want pen and paper. The whole bollocks.

Now he was looking at her. She could feel his smile on her skin.

What will you do? he said. Keep them in a drawer? To look at when we're eighty?

That's it. Tucked under my knickers, she said. Or under the bras at least.

Ok, he said. Only, tied with pink ribbon, mind.

I'll get a red rubber band, ok?

It was, she thought, like they'd both already travelled to another country. One you'd heard enough about – sometimes even wondered if you were there. You looked at the policemen's hats, or the colour of the post boxes, to see if they were different. You realised, even if you got there, you might not know it straight away. He hadn't used the word – unlike others, who had, and hadn't. The usual thing with men, of course: he might be telling the truth if he hasn't opened his mouth. But one day, surprised by peace, she thought, But, this is it, isn't it? It was unexpected to find she'd spoken aloud; less so, that she didn't much care. They each supposed she wouldn't have spoken if there'd been something she'd needed to ask.

The letter

You are walking in the street in a run-down northern city, when you notice a piece of paper in the gutter. Something prompts you to bend down and pick it up, and it is a letter, or the rough draft of a letter – it's hard to tell which. And this is what it says:

Dear Doctor,
Could you please write me out another sick note as the Social
Sercurty have lost the one you gave me last time. They have
asked me to get it back dated from the 5th/9th/**. I always get
a 12 mth sick note. I'd be grateful if you could do this for me.
Also could I have my Inhalers, I have Ventalin & Beckatide.
Also could you arrange to get me to see a Phycaertist please, as
I need to see one as I'm not copeing very well at all without
one & would like to start seeing one again every week or every
two week. Thank you. S. ******
c/o
****
****

Im as skitzerfrenik.
also personaltiy disorder
Asmatic
Deaf in one ear.
Suffer from Depression.

P.T.O.

My files you have sent to H.M. Prison Risley Warrington. They told me if you phone or write they will sent them back to you and youll still be able to give me my sick note until then thankyou. I need my sick note as I'll not get my money until then.

The accident

Whatever you do, she thought, you have to do it as well as you can.

It was a funny thing to come into your head at such a time. She wouldn't have thought she'd think of that.

Rain was falling outside, and you could hear the sounds of traffic too, from the road below. The only thing that was unusual was the man with the thin face who sat in the armchair and looked at her. His arms were crossed loosely in his lap, and he seemed relaxed, as if he had all the time in the world. All the time in the world, she thought. How strange. Is there more time in different places? Could you put it all together? Could you find it if you went to look for it? Once you're falling, they say, everything slows down. So you have plenty of time to regret that mistake; and all the ones before.

The paper dragons

He folded the dragon carefully, studying how to do it from the book he had. It gave him something to do, filled his time, as he lay in bed, one leg covered in white plaster. There were other people in the ward, but it was difficult to chat to them, lying with your leg stuck in the air. They came over to him sometimes, but that was artificial, like having visitors then wanting them to go, not knowing what to say. So he lay on his back and folded paper. A couple of colleagues from work, a man and a woman, had brought the book and the paper – a happier inspiration than he might have thought them capable of, at least individually. But no doubt that was explained by the jointness of the enterprise – just as, no doubt, the same jointness made it easier for them to endure the boredom – the awkward journey, the awkward visit. In fact he somehow suspected – he wasn't sure why – that it had worked out even happier for them than that. That a dutiful visit to a convalescing colleague allowed them an out-of-office – and extra-marital – excursion that neither might otherwise have had quite the courage to suggest. He wondered – to put it crudely – how long the visit was supposed to have gone on – or maybe how difficult the traffic had been, or the hospital to find – and whether other dutiful visits were supposed to have followed.

In reality, like the others from other colleagues and acquaintances, it had been brief and unrepeated – a fact that did not surprise him or at all dismay him. He preferred to avoid awkwardness; and if that involved the understanding that he lacked friends, that was no surprise, since he knew he lacked the lust for friendship. If he thought about it, he had known, as a child, the longing to love and be loved; but that had not survived the more urgent demands of adolescence. He had known, as an adolescent, the longing to be known; but that had not survived the adult recognition of its futility – or the even more adult recognition of its undesirability. He had known, as a young man, the longing for shared laughter; but that had not survived the tedium of no longer being young. And he had known, of course – how to escape? – the images of perfection, both physical and emotional; and had sought to survive these by choosing such imperfect relationships as he could always leave behind.

There was, he'd wanted to think, an ounce of compassion in this, if a hundredweight of convenience. The way he lived – the way he was – whichever it was – he'd never felt he had the power to sustain a woman's love for very long. By choosing such couplings as failed to arouse much emotion in him, he somehow hoped to lessen the harm, by failing to arouse it in the other. In practice, of course, it merely meant he harmed people that he didn't care about. How far one survived on that basis – or how far one merely survived – and – more to the point – how far the ultimately abandoned others survived – who were likely to have had different perspectives on the matter – these were issues of which he was well enough aware, when he wanted to be. The reality was, he'd always found it easy to be honest with himself, and easier still to be dishonest with others. And if that meant that he lay by himself, folding paper dragons, well, he might at least hope that did little harm. Even if – if his suspicions were correct – he had merely advanced from being an agent of deceit, to an occasion of deceit in others...

And so gradually, while he thought, he folded many things: flowers, fish, stars, and dragons, most of all dragons. And gradually people – nurses, patients, visitors – began to pause at his bedside to look at them for a moment, and nod to him, and smile. And children, of course, too, when they came to other beds at visiting time. He knew nothing of children, had no interest in them. But gradually he found quiet ways to let them look, and choose, and pick up, and turn and look at him, and for him to nod, and them to clutch, and turn, and scamper off in delight. And – more difficult, but he made a beginning – quiet ways to accept the smiled thanks of their parents, and to give just the right smile and conspiratorial nod in return.

And then, when he was healed, and home, he wondered if somehow he could continue. Find a circumstance in which all of this might still seem natural. There was a park where he loved to walk, and where people flew kites on Sundays. And so gradually he made a habit of going there, to the hill where there were people all around, and letting the dragons and their companions sit on the bench beside him, while he folded more – with, in time, the same happy results. And in winter, or if it was wet, he sat in the café, and they came to know him and didn't mind. And gradually the quietness spilled out around him, as people paused, and stood, and watched. And if he never learnt to meet their eyes, at least he learnt how to make it so they did not notice. And sometimes he would look up and – in the gaps in the clouds and the sunlight – or off through the trees and hedgerows – almost think that he could see dragons.

On the road

On the road, nothing was moving. The road ran back almost straight, to the very far distance; only in places it seemed to change width suddenly, where a rise and fall broke the line of perspective. Then it was abruptly lost, at the foot of the last line of hills.

The hitch-hiker had left his pack sitting at the edge of the asphalt, and was standing leaning his chest against a solitary roadsign, letting the metal take his weight, watching back down the road. Behind him, just ahead, the road made a bend among the olive trees, before beginning to climb gradually towards the next pass. It was mid-morning, and already there was the strange stillness of very hot days. Off to the left, among the trees, a flock of sheep moved slowly over the ground, the bell of the leader tolling steadily.

The hitch-hiker stirred, and watched the earth at his feet. An engine could have been heard for miles. Two or three ants were busy, making their way over the red surface. Feeling the dryness in his mouth, the hitch-hiker spat to one side – and saw the face of a pebble suddenly darken, where the saliva had struck. He wondered how he had changed the lives of the creatures that lived on that stone. Killed them? or given them a medium to flourish in? He remembered a sentence he'd once read: we crush out thousands of existences, every step that we take.

Off among the trees, the sheep were moving steadily closer. The hitch-hiker yawned, and glanced back down the road; then looked again at the ground at his feet. One of the ants was scrabbling over the surface, just beneath. If the hitch-hiker opened his mouth, and let saliva fall again, perhaps he would trap the creature in a gob of spittle. He suddenly felt very interested, in seeing what would happen. Would the ant drown? No, maybe not. But remnants of the saliva might slowly eat at him; condemn him horribly. Did insects feel pain as we did? he wondered. He didn't know. Perhaps nobody did.

He still felt curious; but he straightened up, and moved away.

Suddenly he wondered if God was like that. Curious, forgetful. Tired and fitful. Uncertain and powerless and too strong.

No. Sometimes he almost understood how one believed in a God. But in the end it was not a powerful idea – not so powerful as the idea of chance. Will, love, and need. And then chance.

It was getting warm; nothing was moving on the road. The hitch-hiker sat on the earth by the roadside, by his pack. He rubbed his face. It was utterly peaceful. The sheep's bell rang.

The gift

There was once a baby born into an unhappy family. And so, when he was twenty-four, he was an unhappy man. Knowing a little of himself, he had left his world of dead knowledge, in search of sun and laughter. But people stayed divided into four classes. Those you desired. Those on whom you impressed your mind. Those who kept the universe away with shared humour. And those who took the women you wanted, thought you a fool, and preferred not to laugh at your jokes. One day, travelling in a poor country, he came across a hunchback dwarf, knocked down and dying in the road. Knowing a little of the language, and the customs of human beings, the young man knelt down, and offered him water from a flask. No, no, said the dying one, in good English, pointing to his pack with the last of his energy: We have wine. We can drink to our health.

The young man bit his lip, and froze a little more of his soul. He knew that life couldn't love him, it thought him dwarfed in spirit. But did it need to mock him through the mouth of someone, who should have been too busy leaving it?

Being young somewhere

The call to prayer woke him early. He went out to fetch breakfast. The great square almost empty now. Used schoolboy French, brought back milk, bread, figs.

She ate and then threw up again.

He sat on the bed and rubbed her back. "It was your turn to be pregnant, at least," she said.

In her mouth, his language became a way of telling the truth.

She cried for a bit, lay down among the sleeping bags.

"When can we make love again?" she said.

"When it's certain."

She made a sound. "It's certain now," she said.

He went and got a bucket, so she could wash in the room. Downstairs, in the café, the music was starting. Some others going down, rucksacks packed, moving on.

When she was dry, she sat on the bed, just in her red socks, and brushed her hair. She was finding flakes, soap or dandruff, she couldn't tell.

"I think I get bald," she said.

"So I'll sell you. Get a camel. Maybe two."

So many things not to want in this world. Or maybe not the way he'd offered them.

She jabbed at him with the brush, and he grinned and dodged. Then grabbed the brush, and made to run the bristles down her left breast.

She crossed her arms and smiled.

"Not to piss about," she said.

In the bar

The man sat in the bar, and around him people giggled, eyeing him and giggling – or at least the women did. He sat and considered the reason for the giggling. They were foreign women in this foreign country; not bar girls, he'd say, but ordinary working girls, mostly in groups together. Were they giggling then like girls back home might do, laughing at their lives, or him, or nothing? Or were they giggling from embarrassment? He knew, people in these countries sometimes giggled from embarrassment. And was the embarrassment that he might talk to them? Or that he might not? Or – more likely – that they didn't know what he might do, being a stranger and strange. Were some giggling as a girl might do with a man, out of shyness, before whatever else begins, to fill up the time before it begins? Which is another kind of embarrassment, but a nicer kind. Or were they giggling because they were hard working and hard worked, and it was evening, and the weekend, and work was over, and it was time to live and not dream, so that our dreams can find us, but dreams don't live in bars, and so perhaps they were giggling because, if they didn't, well, then, everything might just seem very sad indeed.

The exile

He went to the local women for sex, watched television to imagine love. Then lay awake and listened to his life; for these were not what he missed.

Outside the bedroom, you couldn't tell, down here. Hidden by wall or cloth; or if not, you mustn't look. But you saw it, he thought; three or four times in your life. In real life, that was. Not dreams, or – dream machines. And you knew it when it happened – because they were the ones you couldn't *not* look at. Oh, you managed to, of course, because you didn't want to make a fool of yourself. And anyway it's rude to stare. But it was all you could do, that turning away; it was on the very edge of effort. And you could still feel the pressure, off to one side, or behind you, where they were. And it wasn't just you, it was the same for everyone; you could tell by the tension in the air. And there had been all the others, of course. The ones you fancied. And the ones men clustered round. And the ones who somehow lit up a room. And the ones you fell in love with. But these, these few, they were different. It had nothing to do with chatting up, or winning, or loving, or living with. That was all.. unimaginable. It had nothing to do with normal life. And so.. he supposed... it must be.... that it was about beauty. Just that. All by itself..! As if for a moment that really was there. Not fashion – or genetics – or psychology – or biochemistry – But really there. Eternal and warm and unchanging. And reaching out for a moment to touch human life.

Other lives

When he was young, he'd hitch-hiked to a cheap warm country for the winter. Down in the south there was a village, where other travellers came to camp on the beach. Not far back from the beach was a pool, a little concrete-edged reservoir that filled with fresh water, good for cooking and washing. It irrigated the ground where the villagers grew vegetables, so you had to be careful not to get soap in the pool itself. One day he was washing there, stripped down to his pants, when he heard a stone fall close to him. He looked up, and saw two village children a little way off, up on a bluff overlooking the pool. Tending sheep or goats, probably; one had a stick in his hand. He thought at first they were angry, though he was careful not to get soap in the water. But then he saw they were pointing. He turned, and saw a black snake just behind him, where he had been about to step.

He stepped away, turned to wave his thanks, and then the children were gone. Afterwards he wondered if that was one of those moments when your life was changed. You always knew that, hitch-hiking. A different lift, and your life could be different. But sometimes it was stronger; you could feel another universe splitting away. Like one time in Ireland, on holiday, alone, on the wet west coast, standing on a high rock cliff overlooking the Atlantic. He'd turned, and come too close to a great funnel in the earth, dropping down to a sea pool far below. He'd known it was there, but he'd got too close all the same. Always afterwards he felt like another world had been hatched at that moment, one where he'd fallen and been killed or drowned. He imagined his parents gradually realising they hadn't heard from him, some of his belongings turning up in the empty out-of-season hostel where he'd stayed, the grief, the uncertainty ever after unless his body was found. A feeling so strong, he felt guilty, about this other world his carelessness had created. He couldn't shake the feeling that it had really happened; that he'd spawned another universe, in which people who'd loved him lived a life of grief.

Now, back by train from his own son's funeral, he sat in the town in the fast-food place, sheltering from the evening, waiting for the last bus, watching people passing in the street outside. The piped music filling his head, the beat beginning to calm him. Sitting at the table, his chin on his hand, his elbow on the table, his other arm stretched out along the cushioned back of the bench. The beat of the music gradually spreading through him, not his music, but hypnotising the mind, locking him into stillness as the people passed. The two or three women, turning and joking. The young man pausing for a moment to draw on a cigarette, then moving off again. A mother with a child on her chest. The beat of the music building up, till he felt he could sit there motionless for ever. And he, he thought, an old man, muttering in the street.

How it is

He was remembering a time when the ducks had come knocking. There were more of them down at the stream that spring, perhaps ten, rather than four or five. And too many drakes, so they squabbled over the females, squabbled over the food. His wife, she'd started taking them scraps down; not natural, but that was up to her. So next thing, one morning, there'd been a tapping on the kitchen door. He'd opened it, and there they were, a delegation of ducks, in line ahead, ducklings in tow, looking for food; the leader had been beating on the door with his beak. The cat would have had a fine time of it, if he hadn't stopped her. They hardly knew what they were any more.

And men, he thought. We used to make our minds out of the land, or out of the water. Or maybe, for a time, iron and fire and stone. Now, they try to make their minds out of the air. The phones and the radios and the televisions, and the music players and the modems. What they hear and what they see, the voices and the prices. But you can't make your mind out of air, all the flutter and the flicker, it's too thin; you can only make it out of earth or water. Earth's best for a man, but water will do. And that's why they talk and talk, and turn and turn. Because it's only air, it's all they know, and it can't fill the emptiness inside.

The hook of the sea

He was just shifting the tether of his harness from the port jackline to the starboard when the wave crashed into the cockpit and washed him out of it. He felt himself lifted over the lifelines, bounce once on the hull, then slip into the broken surface of the sea. So this was how it happened, he thought; this was how it came at last. The water began to fill his mouth as he tried to breathe. Then the next wave lifting, and he was back in the cockpit again – sprawled on a locker, the seawater draining out the scuppers. Twisting hard, he grabbed a stanchion, found the tether with his other hand, and clipped it on – then swung back round and grabbed the helm, spewing water from nose and mouth. How unlikely was that? he thought, as he turned the bow back to meet the storm; nobody would believe you. The sea took you, and spat you out.

His whole life hadn't flashed before him; perhaps he'd escaped too early for that. Instead it was just one evening that had come into his head. He'd been young, not yet thirteen, they'd been on holiday in the west country, and his parents had arranged for him to go out on a fishing trip one night. Just him and an older boy, the son of the people who ran the guest house. The older boy didn't want him along, but there was nothing he could say. They'd gone out in a rowing boat, into the calm bay between the headlands. The water lapped gently, and there was moonlight enough to see. The fishing was simple; they each had a line with hooks every few inches. The local boy showed him how to bait each hook with a lugworm, pushing the barb through the body twice. Then they just held the lines out by hand over the sides. After a few minutes they lifted them again, and he couldn't believe it. Most of the hooks had a fish attached – not very big, but big enough. They'd unhooked the fish, and thrown them in the bottom, where they flapped a while. Then re-baited the hooks, and done the same again. It was so easy, even he could get it right.

Then he'd realised the older boy had stopped, and was staring off to the side, not moving. He held up his hand; sit still, his hand said. So he'd just turned his head quietly and looked, and could see a dark shape in the water, like the long underside of an upturned boat. The two of them had sat motionless watching. The whale slowly drifted closer. Perhaps it's asleep, he wondered, perhaps it's dead. Then the spell broke. It was getting too close. The local boy shipped the oars, and started to pull away. The whale stirred, gave the water a slow slap with its tail, and moved off. The older boy had looked shaken, but he, he'd been too innocent for fear. He'd sat and watched in the moonlight, as the whale headed back to sea.

How to kill a chicken

First, you choose one that's not laying, and not scratching for food. That's easy. You went to a farmers' market to get more hens and made a mistake. Bought three white ones and hitch-hiked back with them in a sack. Then realised they were ex-battery. Too old, 'laid out'; and didn't know how to scratch for grubs. Just stood around disconsolately, waiting to be fed. So you chase one of them, catch it, and take it out of sight of the other hens. Hold it to your chest, till it quietens. Tell it that in some future life you give it the right to kill you for food. Then hold its head and wrench it round. You hate it when they run frantic with broken necks, you don't trust the scientists' ideas of death. So you wrench the head right round till it comes off. It's not worth hours of plucking, so you just skin and chop. In minutes it's ready for the pot. You know that sooner or later you'll kill the cockerel. Cheaper to buy day-old chicks than keep him fed. But for the moment his beauty keeps him alive.

A few weeks later, you have friends coming for a meal. Time for him to go. You decide to use an axe but it doesn't go so smoothly, he screams as you begin. Next day, when you serve him up, you say, There you are – *Coq au vin* with real cock.

Years later, when you're getting a few twinges in your back and neck, you're always wary, seeing osteopaths and such. You know that, sooner or later, you're going to meet up with one, who used to be one of your chickens.

Waiting

The car came down the road, and he stepped out of the way, and the car went past and on and out of his life. He had a face that was strange somehow, and thick bushy hair, so people smiled a little to themselves when they saw him. And then, when they knew more about him, they smiled to each other in another way. And he walked on and thought about the car, and how it had gone out of his life and he hadn't even noticed the colour. But how it could have been differ-ent – how he might not have stepped out of the way, or how it might have skidded and come at him, or it might have stopped and the driver been a beautiful woman and lost and needing help. Or it might have been a policeman, a de-tective, and he might have arrested him for something he'd never done, like killing someone or importing drugs or something, and he might never have been able to prove his innocence. Only none of those things had happened and the car had gone on, and so he walked on. Sooner or later, perhaps, something out of the ordinary would happen. He knew that ordinary things probably would not happen for him, because the world usually kept those for people who seemed like other people – even if he could sometimes tell they were really different underneath. But things that were out of the ordinary, they could happen; and maybe he could make do with those.

He was heading towards somewhere where they'd given him work before. It wasn't far now, he'd probably walk through the night. The evening sun at his back made his shadow fall long in front of him; the limbs elongated, the head small and distant, like our dreams of alien life. After a time he came to a village. There were some children coming the other way. They nudged each other when they saw him, tugged on the shoulders of others to turn and look. Hello, they said, pretending to be polite, as he went by; then laughed and shouted after him. Cowards, he thought. He wished he could go back at night and cut their eyes out. But the angels wouldn't sing to him if he thought like that. They were only children, learning to be rude; you had to have compassion. You had to have compassion for everyone except yourself.

The parents of the nightmare

She was frightened that she might be pregnant. If she'd been single, it would have been ok. She would have gone and got it terminated, and her heart wouldn't have hurt too much. But she was married, happily married, and had only ever been with her husband. And that was what made her afraid. It should be a matter of joy, starting your first child; but in this place it didn't bring you peace. She'd seen them, sometimes in town, but mostly in the hospital – when she'd gone with her sister, to hold her sister's hand. What you saw there, what had come out of human wombs, were things you would not want in your dreams. Some with limbs thin and long like insects, or swollen up like those of elephants. Some with legs turned backwards, or no legs at all. Some with heads lolling, their mouths drooling; others always moving, their bodies twitching, their arms jerking in the air. Even the best were gaunt, with shaven heads, dying of hidden cancers. And the most fearful, perhaps, those with balloons of flesh outside their bodies, or their heads, holding their insides or their brains. Her sister's child was there, and they knew that he was dying. Her sister held him to her and wept, and begged God to let him live. And that was what was frightening in this land, now that it was poisoned. Not just what you might bring into this world, or how pitiable its suffering; but if your heart could contain the desperate love.

Lying in the sun

It's 1949 and you're five years old and you're lying in the road in the sun. There's a man standing near you, the father of your friend, a boy the same age as you. And the man, he's asking about what he's just been told. How you and your friend were in a barn with a girl you know, when one of the farm workmen walked in. And the three of you were only standing there, several feet apart; but the girl was holding her skirt pulled up, and her pants pulled down. And so the farm man's told him about it, your friend's father; and now he's trying to ask you. And you're just lying there, face down, head turned away, saying nothing, in the quiet roadway outside your friend's house; feeling the warmth of the tarmac on your chest, and the warmth of the sun on your back. You don't feel at all concerned about what's happened; and you don't feel at all worried about what might happen – you can probably hear the uncertainty in the man's voice. And indeed the man knows very well kids do this sort of thing from time to time; he did much the same when he was your age, then pretty well forgot about it, till adolescence came along. So he's going through the motions, not wanting to make much of it – not wanting the embarrassment of talking to your parents. And you, what you feel, is this incredible feeling of power, over an adult. Because he's not your father, and there's nothing he can do to make you talk. So you just lie there in the roadway, saying nothing; feeling this great strange feeling of power filling your body; and the warmth of the tarmac; and the wonderful warmth of the sun.

94

The woman in white

It was in the dark before dawn that he saw the woman walking across the water. There was only a thin moon, and no lights in the village ashore. But he could see her walking towards him, her face and clothes white against the darkness. For a moment he thought it was his wife, as if she'd died and come to tell him – or wanted to warn him that a child was ill. He'd only been out that night, but who knew what might have happened? – a sudden sickness, a scorpion, a snake. Out there it had been quiet enough, in the little boat, guarding the end of the tunny line. His lamp had failed, but there'd been the moon, and the pulse of light beyond the headland, and his packet of cigarettes to see him through. But now there was the woman, coming on, till he saw it was no-one he knew, not even one of his people. Then she stopped, and looked at him, and pointed to the sea beyond.

He started, lifted his head, turned, and saw the faranji sailboat coming straight at him. He rose up, shouted, grabbed an oar, beat hard on his boat's hull. A face appeared, looked startled, as if caught dozing, saw him, saw the dark shoreline, disappeared, and the sailboat turned out to sea. He watched it, then turned around, and the woman too had vanished. These faranji, he thought; they play with the sea as if it didn't mean to kill you. Still, someone had come a long way to save someone, even if it hadn't been him.

Heartland

The rain had been falling for forty days. Not nights. At night it stopped, like a tap turned off. But then a mist rose off the ground and hid the stars, and shut people back up with their thoughts. The earth had been dry, and it was a steady, gentle rain; so, so far, it seemed like a blessing. Crops were growing, reservoirs filling, the meadows were green. And everything else was still familiar. The crow of cockerels, the cough of tractors, the sounds of cattle climbing to the fields in the mornings. Only, people's eyes seemed to peer out, washed of colour, and their faces washed of zest. At dusk, before the mist came, they could see the trees on the hill-sides, lone silhouettes against the sky, as if the past was looking down. For generation on generation the land had brought forth people and buried them. Their bones had built up in the churchyards until the churches seemed sunk in the ground. They'd seen wars and plagues and famines – and still turned the earth to their purpose. But if the land was changing, they might be a crop that ceased to thrive.

The silence

It happened in the dead of winter. The trappers were away in their cabins, and it would be months before the lake melted. This was long before the ice roads; to the south, depression gripped the land. Those in the settlement drank homebrew, and waited for the spring.

Then out of the cold came a sled, pulled by just two dogs; the dogs starved, almost finished, on bleeding feet, the man half frozen into place. So they took him, got his blood flowing, gave the dogs water and food and tried to save them too. They knew who he was, recognised him – he set his traplines in the bear country up north. And eventually he told them how he'd been heading back with two companions, with their furs, when one morning the world had changed. The snow had hung in the air without falling, and there'd been no sounds around them; not from the trees, or the sleds, or even from the throats of the dogs. Only they thought they could hear the sound of ravens calling. And their own voices were still there, just, far away, as if coming from the ends of the earth.

So – as he told it – they'd stopped and looked at each other, and then gone on. Though it was hard to tell the way, everything seemed strange in the hanging snow. Only, after a time his companions began to turn, and head off into the trees, shouting that they could see the lights of home. And he'd caught them and brought them back, but they'd veered off again and again, until they were gone. And then it was just him and the silence and the hanging snow, while the dogs had broken one by one. And he had cut them out and left them, and gone on, till at last he came out of the bear country, and down to the lake shore to the town.

And none of this, of course, made any sense, even as a story. For he was saying how they were coming back for the Christmas trading: when trappers brought the early thick pelts in, and restocked for the leaner months ahead. Only – this was February; though he hardly seemed to know it, that left almost two months unaccounted for. So most of those who heard the story smiled, or shrugged, and wondered what had really happened. Had he killed his companions? or somehow – by accident or negligence – or choice – let them die? Had he holed up in his cabin? or some empty one along the way? Had he caught enough fish, or been lucky and found caribou? or had he – and his dogs – lived on the dead? All of which was why the authorities took him for a time – and then left him well alone. For though they sent a patrol up, there was nothing to be seen or proved. So that was the consensus, and only a few wondered and said nothing. Saying nothing being simplest, in this world of joke and take. But – why tell a story if it only causes questions? – there was that, of course. And then – how do you say, you've seen something in someone's eyes? or know what it is you've seen? Or what he's known that has put it there?

Back of beyond

One night he brought a woman back to the house. She was a woman of the street, and what they made was not love. Afterwards he got the old van going again, and took her back to the town. Then came back and sat and listened to the house. They did not want him in the Church any more; but that did not mean he was a fool. The village was on a moorland road, rising to grey crag to one side. The house had been the priest's house, back when the village had had a priest. Now he was supposed to tend it, stop it becoming a ruin, while they decided what to do with it, and him. He had not brought the woman to the room where the priest had lived, still with its crucifix and narrow bed. He had only used that for a couple of nights, and then got out with his thoughts. The second morning, there'd been a pounding on the house door, and when he'd gone there'd been no-one there. That had been enough. He'd moved his few things to the other end of the building, longer disused. There was some furniture there, still good enough, and he'd made up a snug hide against the cold. That was where he'd brought the woman, and that was where he sat and listened. Well, you could call it listening, though it didn't usually come to that. He wasn't a fool; or, not that kind of fool, anyway. He knew very well what kinds of things come to watch, when they smell sex without love.

The stalker

He'd noticed her in the crowded road, and begun to follow. Her clothes, her face, the way she held her body. They told him all he needed about her life.

He followed her along the road, followed still as she turned into the quiet street. He could see the years around her like a dark light.

She knew he was there now, quickened her pace to hurry. He lengthened his stride to close in.

Time to get this done. She'd never meet his eyes, in her fear. The touch of her was all there could be.

He closed right up, sensed her stiffen. Then reached out and clasped her neck. He felt her body jerk with shock.

Then he strode on, leaving her behind; knowing she wouldn't know what had happened. Understanding how it must be. The sudden lightening inside, the joy, the ease spreading through her body. Thinking it was because he'd been right there, upon her; and then he'd walked away.

He strode on, turned down another street, tasting the city in his throat. He was drained. He needed to get to his room and sleep.

There'd been years of this, there'd be years more, he didn't know how many.

For this was purgatory, though the living didn't know it. To go about the world, feared and alone, forgiving the sins of others. Wiping clean in them precisely those sins, for which you yourself had been condemned.

At least, it was for him. He knew we each decide our own payment, even if we don't know it. And he wondered what kind of god he carried in him, that his purgatory was this.

The accursed

The house was at the end of the world, where the land ended and the water began. It was a small house for such a particular place; but big enough for its inhabitants, since they numbered just two, an old man and a boy. I don't know how the boy came to be there, and neither did the boy. For him, of course, it was only natural, having no memory or comparison to show him otherwise. And the old man did not see any need to disturb the natural with explanation. So they lived side by side, the old looking after the young and then, increasingly, the young looking after the old. They had food, and fuel, because people brought them. And again, to the boy, this seemed of course only natural; and again, the old man saw no reason to explain. And why in fact it was – whether from duty, or compassion, or guilt, or love, or even possibly fear – and whether out of regard for the past, or the present, or the future – well, there was a village, and people, and some of them old enough to know. And any of them might have told a stranger, who happened to ask. Or then, again, they might not.

The forger

He was painting, copying the work of a master. It was a painting of a hawk. Of all God's creatures, this was his favourite. The pent ferocity, the sullen beauty. The painting had been growing slowly for days, and now it was almost done. A touch to a feather there, to a claw there; there to the glint in an eye. He stepped back, and looked again, between his work and the original. Caught it? Yes. Yes, it was done.

He left the canvas on the easel and went to the door and looked out over the hard land in the sunlight. Closed the door, went to his bed, and slept.

Two days later, the painting was dry. He took it from the easel and carried it outside. Holding it in front of him, he breathed on it.

The hawk rose from the canvas, shuddered before him, and stretched its wings. It looked him in the eye once, and was gone.

He took the ruined canvas back into the house, and threw it to one side. That had been a kind of holiday. Now it was time for serious work again.

He opened the storeroom door, and carried back in the model, the stuffed dead body of the hawk that he had caught. He chose another piece from his collection, and brought it out. He stood it in place, then chose a tall narrow canvas and placed it on the easel. Very carefully, he began to sketch the outline of a man.

The archipelago of the dead

You never felt fear at sea; but you did, sometimes, feel horror. You don't know why you didn't feel fear. As innocent, as inexperienced as you were – as foolish as you were – you knew that the sea could break you in an instant. Probably it was just the limits of your experience. Your only real storm, you worked below, keeping the hot drinks and the hot food flowing. A tricky enough job! – but shielded from the full fury outside. And then, in the aftermath, when you helmed the boat, then the heavy seas had a rhythm, that carried you. The others might be sleeping below, and you could feel the boat under your hand, rising hard like an elevator to one wavetop, then falling in a plunging slide back down again. And in that downward surge you could feel that, if you were to die out there, well, it would be worth it, a good way to go.

But that was when the boat was alone with the sea. The horror came when you met what wasn't sea. You might feel a stirring of it even at the sight of land, running with the wind down a distant shore of barren cliffs. Or again out in the ocean, if your path crossed that of a cargo ship, coming too close, dwarfed by the great towering hull. But the worst, by far, was when you were closing on the land but couldn't see it yet, and you came across the far outer marker buoy of an estuary, huge and rusted and alone, looming out of the water, perhaps tolling a bell. Even long after, that could make you shudder. Perhaps the ugly meeting of worlds broke the cocoon, exposing you in all your frailty to the truth of what you were playing with. Or maybe it was something else. As if something human, built for an alien environment, and left alone out there, became utterly inhuman; a token of death. Like those great concrete sea forts left over from the war, glimpsed from the sunlit beach where you played your childhood games of castles or battleships. Little distant grey shapes, that couldn't touch a world of paddling pools and donkey rides. And probably long ago destroyed; but in your mind, you can see them more clearly now. The great sea-darkened walls, the dank spaces within. So that now perhaps, seeing them small and distant from the shore, they would seem to be not guarding this world, but marking the way to another. Just over the horizon, a dotted line of grey islands, an unseen archipelago of the dead.

The wide world

He lay on his back and stared at the sky. Clouds stretched above him, white clouds moving in stately procession across a clear blue sky. The sun warmed his skin, birds chattered, a rat rustled among the reeds. The clouds became ships, human heads, wild animals. He thought of the old woman's stories, how there were places where the land rose up and hid the sun. You could look up, she said, and see land instead of sky. Before, there'd been his mother's stories, and he'd understood those. But the Old Ones had taken her down to their home under the sea. He'd seen the boatmen take her body out, and when they'd come back he'd been alone. And now there was the old woman, and her mouth of broken teeth. He trusted the old woman; but he didn't believe her; how could land rise up? Land was like the sea; it was what lay at the bottom of the sky.

The creation myth of the marsh people

In the beginning, the whole world had been made by the Father. He had made the water, and the land, and the sky, and the sea, and fire, and rain, and the sun and stars. But throughout the world there was no living thing. For all the things that he had made were separate from each other, each in one place, the land there and the sea there and the sky there and the water there. Nothing could mix with any other thing; for the Father could give them only their own natures. So everything was empty. And Muna, the Mother, saw this, and wept. And her tears fell throughout the Universe. And wherever her tears touched, they mingled with that thing, and softened it, so each ran to meet its opposite, and chaos and life were born. And out of chaos came every living thing, made of bone and flesh and blood and breath. And also every growing thing, made of earth and death and sun and rain. And Muna's tears melted the Father also, so that from her womb came humanity. And when he saw the first men, his children, he was angry, and wished to kill them; for they were ugly to his eyes. But the Goddess begged him to let them live. So Padu, the Father, prophesied for mankind, saying: You will be of two natures, always uneasy, growing from what is impure, seeking always what is pure. And Muna prophesied and said, You will be of two natures, knowing only your own hearts, but longing always to share the hearts of others. And so the world began.

The notice

It wasn't much of a yacht harbour. Just a corner of the port, with a breakwater to the sea, and water slicked with oil. But it had a toilet block, and showers, and a notice board, and a little outdoor bar ringed with chairs. And one day a new notice appeared on the board: a photocopied sheet, from a family in France. Asking if anyone had seen their daughter and son-in-law; who'd set out to cross the Atlantic the previous year, from where you are, and never been heard of again. Only, just before they set out, they'd taken on two men as crew; and later their credit card was used, once, in Brazil.

And the family have to do what they are doing, of course. They have to photocopy, and send out, and hope. But they know what has happened, and anyone who reads it knows. And now you carry the same images in your head. Two-thirds of the way across, say; a small boat in an empty ocean. The man, no doubt, already dead. The woman, no doubt, for the moment, still alive. And death is death, and so perhaps all deaths should seem the same; but they do not. And some, of people that we have known, leave us untouched; and some, of strangers, haunt us for the rest of our lives.

The moondreamer

Almost every night, when he lay down to sleep, the old man dreamed of the moon. He lay down, and the dreaming began. He could see the moon slipping like a silver coin through the dark pocket of the night. Sometimes his dreaming was strong, and he dreamed of the entire moon, round and shining. Sometimes he could only dream of a part of the moon. And sometimes, when he was at his weakest, he could dream of no moon at all. He was very old, and his strength ebbed and flowed with the weeks, and so his dreams ebbed and flowed. And all round the world, how people saw the moon, depended on his dreams. For he was the man who dreamed the moon. And when he could only dream it a little, it was only a thin crescent in the sky. And when he could dream it all, it was full and round and huge, the queen of the night. And he was very old, but he could not leave his work, because no-one else could dream the moon; though for centuries he had searched for someone, he had never found anyone else who could do it, or would do it, give up their lives to this work. And so of course he went on. Because if he did not dream the moon, there would be no moon. And if there was no moon, then, what pity would there be, in the world?

Going hence

You're watching a TV play. It's about the early lives of that famous comedy duo.

"What's that?" "A Greek urn." "What's a Greek urn?" "About thirty bob a week."

Later, in the middle of the night, your father starts calling.

"Please help me. Please help me. Oh, please help me."

You roll off your mattress on the floor, and go over on your knees. You rest your forehead on his bed and close your eyes.

"What is it?"

No answer. You open your eyes.

"What is it?"

He looks at you. "What's Egypt?"

"Is it your leg?"

"What?"

"What's hurting?"

He looks puzzled. "Is it exciting?"

You rest your forehead back on the bed. You should be holding his hand but you don't think of that.

"Is anything else hurting?"

"Yes it is."

You get upright and go and get some water. Then you crank up the head of the bed and open the painkillers.

"Open your mouth."

"What?"

"Open your mouth. Open wide."

"Pork pie??"

Not long after, he's back in hospital. He's got blood clots on his lungs, and heart arrhythmia, and a scan shows changes to the blood vessels of his brain.

He lies in bed and now you hold his hand.

"Lord let thy," he says. "Lord, let thy. Lord, let thy."

"According to my percy," he says. "My percy. My percy. My percy."

After

The village lay in a fold of the land, with the sun shining on it. The sounds of people and animals rose up.

He turned and walked on. Each day, still, he tried to walk up the ridge a little way. No-one knew why, now; especially him.

The girl ran on, came back, and he stopped again.

Wait a bit, he said. My legs are older than yours.

How old? she said. But she wasn't listening.

Older than the rest of me, I know that, he said. They poked out of my mother first.

The boy was running towards them, up the hillside.

The king's coming, he said; he was breathing hard.

We know, silly, said the girl. We saw them go with the gun.

The boy stopped and pouted.

Why do they give him the gun? he said.

Just to show, the man said. When he's here, he has power.

He could remember when the last bullet was used. It was a long time ago, and it wasn't a story for them.

The boy frowned. His eyes were bad, but he wasn't stupid. He'd meant: why do something when it's just for show?

He looked at the sky. Will it rain? he said. He was thinking of the feast tomorrow; there'd be a feast.

The man looked at the boy. He might be trouble if he lived, but he wouldn't live to see it.

It'll do what it'll do, said the man. You're more ambitious than your sister. She'll just want fine babies, all born arse last. What you want is a sunny day.

Happier as a dog

The dog came into the pastry shop. It was in a country where you could sit in pastry shops, and have a glass of water as well, or even an ice-cream instead. You ate sitting on tall stools, at little shelves that ran round the walls and around the pillars in the middle. It was a very modern place, with metal and glass and mirrors and dark padded seats, and glass doors that stood open onto the warm street outside. And so the dog came in, and he looked to be part retriever, part setter – well-groomed and well cared for – but with all the long-suffering patience of the one, and none of the zany frolic of the other. And he padded steadily in – nothing hesitant or furtive – glancing sideways at you with mournful solemnity – and padded patiently over to a rubbish bin that stood by one of the pillars. Nose in, nose out. Nope. No discarded pastries. Nothing of interest there. Turned, and padded over to the other rubbish bin, by the other pillar. Nose in, nose out. No. Nothing there either. And still with the same eternal long-suffering air; no change of rhythm; no extra disappointed slump; as if all this was quite unsurprising; too familiar for expectation; just part of the job; no point in getting your hopes up; another day another dollar; his merely a stoic gesture; a labour of Sisyphus; a solemn existential act, in the face of a mindless uncaring Providence; he turned towards the door again, and padded solemnly out. And maybe he had other pastry shops to visit, or restaurants, a regular run. And maybe, like most humans, he was happier having his routine to fill the day. And maybe even, being so human, he'd have been happier as a human. Or maybe, like most humans, he'd have been happier as a dog.

* * *

Notes and acknowledgements

In "Freedom", the idea of "the planet of the lost pens" is stolen – with thanks – from Douglas Adams, *The Hitchhiker's Guide to the Galaxy*.

The title of "Being young somewhere" derives from the final lines of Philip Larkin's poem, "Sad Steps".

And in "Going hence", the Greek urn joke dates back to the days of music hall (vaudeville), but the reference here is to its use in *Eric and Ernie*, the television play about the young Morecambe and Wise, written by Peter Bowker.

In "The letter", the text of the letter is copied exactly from a piece of handwritten paper found discarded in a city street.

In "How it is", the story of ducks knocking on a kitchen door for food is a true one, which I owe to an old school friend, G.K. Philbin. In "The hook of the sea", the opening incident, of being washed overboard and then back, happened to the English sailboat delivery captain Peter Phillips. And in "The woman in white", the incident, again true, of almost running down a little unlit fishing boat off the North African coast at night, I owe to the Irish sailor and sailboat delivery captain, John Petch. True, that is, except for the twist of faranji incompetence that I've imposed on events, for which I hope he will forgive me – for in reality it was vigilance, in noticing a smell of tobacco smoke in the night, that prevented a collision. My thanks in all these cases.

On the other hand, "The creation myth of the marsh people" – which might reasonably be assumed to be a translation, or adaptation, of a genuine tradition – is merely the product of my own disingenuous brain.

I do not know the names of the young people whose fate is considered in "The notice". If anyone should recognise the incident – the time was the early 1980s, their departure point the Canary Islands – then it would be right for them to be remembered here.

Finally, "The parents of the nightmare" owes everything to the images and commentary of *Chernobyl Legacy*, by Paul Fusco. But do not search it out, unless you want an experience that will mark your life.

*

Thanks, disclaimer, gratitude

As a mostly one-person operation, I have fewer people to thank than might be usual – and commensurately fewer to blame. So: my thanks to the cover designer, Emir Orucevic, for working so effectively within the limitations of a very specific brief and delivering a design that has already been widely praised; to Miroslav Avakumovic, for his contribution to preparing the cover files for print; and to the team at booksfactory.co.uk, for the care with which they shepherded this book into its first print edition. While on the blame side, we have myself – solely responsible for the various peculiarities of the text. Two ways of handling dialogue; idiosyncrasies of punctuation; inconsistencies of style (three ways of writing "ok"..?); UK spelling, but US punctuation of speech...? All these are deliberate sins for which I alone must account to the gods of good editing.

Second, a disclaimer: I'd hate anyone to come away from the sea stories with the idea that I was myself in any way a proficient sailor. I was involved in a few ocean-going sailboat voyages, over a very brief period (little more than a year); but was always, by far, the least competent person on board. I did perhaps make some stab at being a sea cook – but only thanks to the lack of any competition for the post. In all other ways, anyone out on Sunday in a dinghy would be likely to have more knowledge and skill than I had, and more feel for the handling of the boat.

Finally – one can't sensibly thank places – but one can, as

a very sporadic writer, be grateful to them. These stories were written on three continents over the course of over 40 years – starting on the island of Crete, and ending in the Norfolk village of Winterton-on-Sea. But most were written between 2000 and 2013; and of the various places where circumstances conspired to help, apart from homes in Norwich and later Winterton, I'm especially grateful to the island of Djerba in Tunisia, and the village of Seleuş, near Sighişoara, in Romania.

*   *   *

If you've enjoyed this book – or if you haven't! – you may wish to leave a review on Amazon.

For more about Grey Dolphin Press, and to order copies of this book in paperback and e-book, please visit greydolphinpress.com

For other writings by David Heidenstam, please visit davidheidenstam.com